Chronos

An Anthology of Time Drabbles

Edited by Eric S. Fomley

D1444271

For Cassy, my better half.

Foreword

Thank you for picking up a copy of *Chronos: An Anthology of Time Drabbles*. Within these pages are ninety-eight hundred-word stories on time, time travel, time dialation, time manipulation, time as a weapon, time as an enemy, and so many more variations. I've a fond love of micro fiction. I feel the power of bite sized stories is often underlooked. Each of these bite sized morsels are full sized stories with a beginning, middle, and end, all focused solely on the theme of time. I hope you enjoy.

One Giant Step

John H. Dromey

"The guidance system and power core are intact, but all of the data-gathering instruments are kaput. Somewhere along the timeline—perhaps millions of years in the past—Temporal Probe One was subjected to extreme pressure that compressed the module to half its former size. We're still trying to determine the exact number of foot-pounds involved but it far exceeds what our antigravity suits can handle. I'm afraid that means no time travel for humans."

"Hold on! The striations in the hull are inconsistent with metal fatigue. One pounding foot inflicted all the damage. Our probe was crushed by a brontosaurus."

John H. Dromey enjoys reading—mysteries especially—and writing in a variety of genres. He's had short fiction published in Alfred Hitchcock's Mystery Magazine, Crimson Streets, Stupefying Stories Showcase, and elsewhere, as well as in a number of anthologies, including Chilling Horror Short Stories (Flame Tree Publishing, 2015) and Drabbledark: An Anthology of Dark Drabbles (Shacklebound Books, 2018).

Your Day Plus One

John Hoggard

I stumbled over @yourdayplus1 when I first joined Twitter and accepted the automatic recommendation without really thinking about it.

As I didn't use Twitter much, save a little, seemingly futile, self-promotion, it was a few weeks, possible months, before I noticed that @yourdayplus1 started Retweeting things from me I hadn't yet tweeted.

Usually these retweets were terrible, relating to the death's of famous people or heart-wrenching disasters which hit the mainstream news twenty-fours hours later.

I was horrified and fascinated.

However, today there's a retweet about my life changing lottery win, so I'm going out now to buy a ticket.

John Hoggard has been writing for as long as he can remember, his first publishing successes coming in the Hartlepool Mail "Chipper Club" aged 6. Since then he's continued to write mainly in the Science-Fiction and Fantasy genres, winning prizes for his "fan-fic" of the Star Trek franchise in his twenties at the various Conventions he attended.

John has also written several pieces of background fiction based on the game Oolite and his most popular work, Lazarus, serialised over 16 weeks, received over 15,500 viewings during that time. The E-book Anthology, Alien Items, featuring some of John's work (writing as DaddyHoggy), was released in early 2012.

In June 2012 John won the Biting Duck Press "Science in Fiction" Short Story Competition.

In November 2012, John's SF short story Baby Babble was included in the Anthology Fusion by Fantastic Books Publishing.

In October 2014 John contributed two pieces of flash fiction to a charity horror anthology, Ten Deadly Tales

In May 2016, John's had two SF short stories All in the Mind and The House was included in the Anthology Synthesis also by Fantastic Books Publishing.

John was most recently published in the horror anthology '666', where his 666-word story 'Headhunted' was highly commended by the editors of the anthology

In November 2017 John had five drabbles in an Official Elite: Dangerous Publication, Elite Encounters by David 'Selezen Lake' Hughes.

In June 2018 John had a drabble accepted into the new Science Fiction Magazine, The Martian Magazine, a new Science Fiction magazine currently specialising in the publication of drabbles.

John's main work in progress is a contemporary novel entitled Endless Possibilities about the world of Online Gaming and Science-Fiction Conventions. He is also working on a collection of 75-word short stories based on his successful contributions to the Paragraph Planet website and is working with illustrator Helen Withington to bring a selection of these stories to life.

Diastanaut

M. Yzmore

Featureless, Imoghen could be anyone. Ze had traveled the multiverse more times than any other diastanaut, yet had never encountered anyone who'd recognized zir. Ze felt untethered, fearless, and that was enough.

One day, the portal glitched. Imoghen thought ze was home, but people looked at zir and smiled. As days passed, Imoghen ran into many whom ze'd met on zir travels, and they all remembered zir. Here, everyone did.

What a strange pocket of the multiverse, thought Imoghen. For the first time, ze felt tethered.

Imoghen decided to stay. Someplace unspeakably remote, after weeks on life support, Imoghen flatlined.

Maura Yzmore writes short-form literary and speculative fiction, as well as humor. Her recent work can be found in Asymmetry, Exoplanet, Occulum, and elsewhere. Find out more at https://maurayzmore.com or on Twitter @MauraYzmore.

Tock

Mike Murphy

Tick!

The dusty mantel clock hadn't peeped since Aunt Beryl. . .

Jake gasped. He would have thrown the cursed thing away long ago if he could only bring himself to touch it.

He clutched his blankets, waiting for the inevitable.

The scream was prolonged: Someone falling down the stairs. Belle! Jake felt shameful relief that he was safe.

She painfully called for his help. If only the damn thing would *tock* it would be safe to go to her. He knew that from experience.

The silent clock mocked him, happily sating its soul hunger while Jake's shame tearfully grew.

Mike Murphy has had over 150 audio plays produced in the U.S. and overseas. He's won five Moondance International Film Festival awards in their TV pilot, audio play, short screenplay, and short story categories.

His prose work has appeared in several magazines and anthologies. In 2015, his script "The Candy Man" was produced as a short film under the title DARK CHOCOLATE. In 2013, he won the inaugural Marion Thauer Brown Audio Drama Scriptwriting Competition.

Mike keeps a blog at audioauthor.blogspot.com.

The Trouble with Time Travel

Patrick Crossen

"March 9th," she said politely.

"Yes of course," I said, trying to remain casual. "And the year?"

I saw the familiar rhythm of muscles in her face begin to tumble slowly downwards.

"Why…it's 1864, dear."

"Of course," I mumbled. "Sorry."

On more than one occasion I'd stumbled into a time that I didn't recognize. That's the trouble with time travel: it's not difficult. Your legs and feet can get you from *here* to *there* of course, but they can also get you from *now* to *then* with ease. So, once more I stepped forward in space and back in time.

Patrick Crossen is a writer from Pittsburgh, PA. He writes sketch comedy, film criticism, and fantasy. When he's not exploring his own fantastic worlds, he's eagerly checking his mailbox for the Hogwarts letter he insists is still on its way.

Good Luck Back There Eve

Stuart Conover

All systems were go for the first jump. The Cronos Class Mark IX would be the first human trial to travel back in time.

Eve could barely contain her excitement. She knew the science was sound, they'd already sent back multiple test animals.

A 10-second countdown.

"..1 Good luck back there Eve."

In the blink of an eye bright light filled the chamber. The room faded from view. The light shot forward and backward in a straight line.

So did Eve.

She opened her mouth in wonder.

The light blinked out.

So did eve.

"..1 Good luck back there Eve."

Stuart Conover is a father, husband, rescue dog owner, horror author, blogger, journalist, horror enthusiast, comic book geek, science fiction junkie, and IT professional. With all of that to cram in on a daily basis, it is highly debatable that he ever is able to sleep and rumors have him attached to an IV drip of caffeine to get through most days.

A resident in the suburbs of Chicago (and once upon a time in the city) most of Stuart's fiction takes place in the Midwest if not the Windy City itself. From downtown to the suburbs to the cornfields - the area is ripe for urban horror of all facets

Homepage: http://www.StuartConover.com

Twitter: http://www.twitter.com/StuartConover

Facebook: https://www.facebook.com/StuartConoverAuthor

Life Sentence

Tianna Grosch

Time can be spent and time can be wasted but mine is nothing if not weighted. Time gets lost and time flies. You can keep time and make time, but you can't defeat or stop it. I've been biding my time while I serve it in this cell – five feet across, eight feet wide. I pace, counting each second dribbling down walls like rainwater. I am condemned – my sentence a lifetime. Dark shadows coalesce in deep corners. Time trickles like grains of sand through spread fingers. I yearn for my escape; somewhere time no longer has its hold on me.

Tianna Grosch has been writing her whole life and received her MFA at Arcadia University last year. Tianna is working on a debut novel about women who survive trauma as well as a memoir. Her work has previously appeared or is forthcoming in Ellipsis Zine, Crack the Spine, Burning House Press, Who Writes Short Shorts, New Pop Lit, Blanket Sea Magazine, Echo Lit Mag and Nabu Review (both lit mags of Paragon Press), among others. In her free time she gardens on her family farm and dreams up dark fiction. Follow her on Twitter @tianng92 or check out her writing on CreativeTianna.com.

Future Tweak

R. Daniel Lester

The man watched the boy walk to school. Poor kid. No idea the hard times ahead. He readied pages full of stock tips and life advice.

Tweak your future to pimp your past.

Stepping from behind the tree: "Hey, kid, I got somethin'--"

But his young self only saw a dirty bearded stranger who'd spent two weeks sleeping in the woods and eating from dumpsters. Time travel ain't as easy as it looks on TV.

The boy kicked his shin, screamed, "Pervert!" and ran away.

On the upside, jail was warm and dry and provided three squares a day.

R. Daniel Lester's writing has appeared in print and online in multiple publications, including Adbusters, Geist, 365 Tomorrows, Broken Pencil, Pulp Literature and the Lascaux Prize Anthology. Recently his novella, *Dead Clown Blues* was shortlisted for a 2018 Arthur Ellis Awards for Best Crime Novella by the Crime Writers of Canada. The second book in the Carnegie Fitch Mystery Fiasco series, *40 Nickels,* will be released in May 2019.

A Wholesome Meal At Hangan's Galactic Fast-food Emporium

Jez Patterson

Originally Published in *Things Unordinary: Volume Three*

"'*Fast food*' is so named because it tastes like it's already half-digested!"

"Not ours," laughed Hangan, placing a single seed on my plate. "Quite the opposite end of the process. Swallow this and a fresh, fast-growing cabbage will instantly grow in your stomach. If you prefer meat, just swallow this egg. And the...well..."

Hangan blushed blue, knowing human sensibilities on this subject.

"What's the point?" I asked. "Humans' enjoyment of eating is all in the taste, the texture."

"Ahh, perhaps you should have thought of *that* before you ate the bourbon shrimp flambé," Hangan said, taking a step back.

Jez Patterson is a teacher and writer currently alternating between the UK and Madrid. Links to other things with his name at the end can be found at: jezpatterson.wordpress.com.

Timing is Everything

Brian K. Lowe

"Did you press my suit, Igor?"

"Yes, master."

"You didn't burn it this time, you incompetent fool?"

"No, master."

"Did you get the coffin polish? I asked you a dozen times."

"Yes, master..."

"You bought rosewood, this time, idiot? Not English oak?"

"Yes...master."

"Good. That English Oak reminds me of... Stop standing around and help me with this cravat—never mind! Get away! Your fingers are like sausages. Peasant..."

"Sorry, master."

"The time is changing! Did you at least remember to reset the clocks? I don't want to go out in the daylight."

"Yes, master. Fall forward, spring back."

Brian K. Lowe is a member of SFWA with over 35 sales, including *Galaxy's Edge*, *Intergalactic Medicine Show*, and *Daily Science Fiction*. By day, he's a paralegal at a small office in Los Angeles.

Single-Speed Upstream

Daniel Pietersen

The thing about time travel is this; you're already doing it. Sure, single-speed downstream basic model time travel that you barely notice, like the 30km/s you're pulling through space just standing there, but still time travel nonetheless. 50 years into the future? It takes 50 years. It's obvious when you think about it. We just didn't. So, sending people back 500 years or whatever, single-speed *upstream*? They just never seemed to get there. Poor devils. God only knows what they thought back then, all these mummified chronos popping into existence. Dead as doornails. Took us 15 years to realise.

Daniel Pietersen writes weird fiction and horror philosophy. He's a contributor to Hippocampus Press' Dead Reckonings journal and his essay on the limit experience in The Hellbound Heart will be published in the imminent second volume of Thinking Horror. He lives in Edinburgh, Scotland, with his wife and dog.

Web: https://constantuniversity.wordpress.com/
Twitter: @pietersender

Starbuckaneers
David Rae

In 2039, we finally unified space and time. Never mind the math; It's really not that complicated. Now we can move to any place and any time in an instant. It's a revolution like no other.

We reached out to the stars and to every planet. We went back in time and stopped all wars and disasters. All time and space unified. That's what we've done.

No matter where you are, or when, you can get a Starbucks or a McDondalds. We've turned the whole universe into a shithole; filled it with empty coffee cups until the end of time.

David Rae lives in Scotland. He loves stories that exist just below the surface of things, like deep water.

He has most recently had work published or forthcoming in; THE FLATBUSH REVIEW, THE HORROR TREE, LOCUST, ROSETTA MALEFICARIUM, SHORT TALE 100 and 50 WORD STORIES. You can read more at Davidrae-stories.com.

The Benefit of Hindsight

Dougas Prince

Eyes open, I stood outside my front door... again.

Upstairs, I hear the two of them fucking away. I should leave, but I don't.

I don't because I can't.

I can't, because I didn't.

Sneaking upstairs, I kick open the bedroom door, like last time and the time before.

I try to stop myself from burying the kitchen knife in her throat, but I can't.

This is how it happened.

This is how it always happens.

I hear my mouth utter those same six words.

"Please, God, let me go back."

Eyes open, I'm stood outside my front door... again.

Douglas Prince is a 28-year-old writer of horror and other dark fiction.

Born in Melrose, Scotland, he now lives on the Wirral peninsula in Merseyside, where he writes stories and reads more books than can possibly be good for him.

Twitter: @darkness_doug

URL: https://theprinceofdarkness.com

Maybe Tomorrow

Jack Wolfe Frost

Bare white walls. I've been here before, yesterday. Or was it a year ago?. I don't know really – I simply remember this place, like a dream. There is no door or windows. Nothing. Perhaps it is tomorrow? Maybe, I just can't say.

I sit on the floor and ponder, as I usually do.

Usually? Do I?

If I knew if it was yesterday, today, or tomorrow I would know more. Maybe tomorrow I will, unless of course tomorrow is yesterday. I remember sounds – once. Children, laughter, and then screams. Perhaps I will again. Now it is white walls.

Maybe tomorrow.

Jack Wolfe Frost is the Eternal Rebel; he rebels against everything which may have the word "rules" or "behave" within it. Born in Sheffield, UK, in 1956; he first started writing in 1982, as a hobby - Now older and wiser, he has had several poems and short stories published.

The Red-Nosed Man

I. E. Kneverday

Years of alcohol abuse had given the man a Rudolphesque nose… but not the power of flight. This was evident from the fact that his body had plummeted straight to the pavement and popped like a piñata upon impact.

As a former Catholic, the act had given me pause. For in pushing the red-nosed man from the rooftop, I had effectively ended my own life as well as his.

While climbing down the fire escape, I whispered goodbye to the confetti remains of my grandfather, then watched in silent awe as the tips of my fingers began dissolving into nothingness.

I. E. Kneverday is a writer of science fiction, horror, and fantasy. His short fiction has been featured in publications including _Drabbledark_, _Exoplanet Magazine_, and _101 Words_. Learn more at Kneverday.com and come say hi on Twitter (@Kneverday) and Facebook (facebook.com/kneverday).

Later

Eric Lewis

I did everything I was supposed to do.

Make friends? Later, got to study.

Ask out that blonde undergrad? Can't, got to run another reaction, get that PhD!

Build credit? Plenty of time after nailing this interview.

Network? Meh, better just keep my head down, hit those metrics.

See a dentist? Why bother, I'll be moving to a better city any day now.

Buy a home? Not with this crappy job I have now!

Get married? Please, who'd want me now with my bald head and beer gut?

Start a family? Don't be stupid, I don't have enough time left.

Eric Lewis is an organic chemist in the New England area, navigating the latest rounds of layoffs and still learning how to be a person again after surviving grad school. His short fiction has been published in Nature: Futures, Electric Spec, Bards and Sages Quarterly, Allegory, Devilfish Review, the anthologies Into Darkness Peering and Best Indie Spec Fiction Vol 1, and other venues detailed at HYPERLINK "https://ericlewis.ink/" https://ericlewis.ink.

Buying Time

CR Smith

Time can be purchased in the underground marketplace. Vials are kept there in glass cabinets under lock and key. You are permitted to look but not touch.

The auction is already underway when we arrive. Several buyers rush passed, a vial hidden about their person — you can tell by the relief etched on their faces.

The bidding is high, the stakes higher. Our offer yesterday was outbid, today's too.

Daily transactions are deliberately limited, inflating the price. With this auction drawing to a close our anxieties heighten.

Ambushing the winning bidder, we shatter their vial and buy ourselves some time.

CR Smith is an artist and writer living in the UK. Her work has been published by Ellipsis Zine, Spelk Fiction, Visual Verse, Zeroflash and The Cabinet of Heed, and is to be found in several anthologies including, The Infernal Clock, Drabbledark: An Anthology of Dark Drabbles and 'Please Hear What I'm Not Saying'. There are also upcoming pieces in the Trembling With Fear anthology, The Infernal Clock Deadcades anthology and the Zeroflash anthology.

The Future Planner

Catherine J. Cole

I think I messed up.

Yesterday, I took action based on the plan I formulated last Wednesday, with the knowledge I gained the previous month using my Future Planner, regarding what would happen a year later counted as of yesterday's date.

The Planner calculates the probabilities of future occurrences based on past experiences I've had, matching them to current events.

It's not that I don't love my invention, it's just that I am eighty-two, and I do believe I maxed out all my credit cards on pleasure a year and two days earlier than my accident is supposed to happen.

Catherine J. Cole won 1st prize in the Metamorphose Literary Science Fiction & Fantasy Short Fiction Contest. The winning story appeared in the anthology *Metamorphose Vol. 2.* More of her short fiction can be found in the magazines and anthologies *Candlesticks and Daggers: An Anthology of Mixed-Genre Mysteries*, *Fantasia Divinity Magazine's Distressing Damsels*, *One Hundred Voices Vol. 3*, and *Broadswords and Blasters Issue 6*. Ms. Cole has lived in the United States, France, and Colombia. When not writing, she works as a translator, which demands that she often work abroad, away from her family in Florida. Follow her on Twitter @CJCole2U and check out her website www.catherinejcole.com.

Where Credit is Due

Joshua Scully

At the completion of another exhausting shift, Jorge pushed his way toward the exit of the lithium processing facility. Twelve hours of battery production had left him with fresh burns from the various mechanized elements of the facility and reeking of brine.

The android at the gateway scanned the code branded onto the back of Jorge's left hand.

"Thank you, Jorge Iturri," the android clicked patronizingly. "Your compensation for today is 200 credits and five minutes. Your available credit balance is now 209 credits and your end day and time is now May 22, 2128 at 8:35am."

Jorge sighed wearily.

Joshua Scully is an American History educator and author of speculative fiction from Pennsylvania. His work can be found on Twitter @jojascully or online at www.jjscully.wordpress.com.

Live a Full Life

Kelly Matsuura

2053. I built a machine. I travelled through time; saw all the unseen.

1965. History took place. Launched high in a rocket, I floated in space.

1912. I forewarned the Titanic. It altered its course and survived the Atlantic.

1889. Adolf Hitler was born. From the book of world horrors, those pages were torn.

1504. For no reason at all: spent two years in China and helped build The Wall.

1991. Made a film in Bombay. Fell in love with a dancer, who begged me to stay.

2056. I wanted to see: how my dear wife now lives without me.

Kelly Matsuura grew up in Victoria, Australia, but always dreamed she would live abroad. She has lived in northern China and Michigan in the US, and over ten years in Nagoya, Japan, where she now lives permanently.

Kelly has published numerous short stories online; in group anthologies; and in several self-published anthologies. Her speculative fiction has been published by *Visibility Fiction, Crushing Hearts & Black Butterfly Publishing, A Murder of Storytellers*, and *Ink and Locket Press*.

As the creator and editor for *The Insignia Series*, Kelly uses her knowledge of Asian cultures to help other indie authors produce great diverse stories and to share the group's work with a new audience.

Blog: www.blackwingsandwhitepaper.com

Facebook: Kelly Matsuura/Kelly Noro Author

Twitter: Kelly Matsuura

The Insignia Series blog: www.insigniastories.com

Selfish Past

Liam Hogan

"Here she is!"

He stares at the girl in the scope. Dr Emily is an expert by now, zooming in on whatever our stream of visitors desperately wants to see.

"Go on, lover boy!" she encourages with a wave.

Blushing and grinning like an idiot he steps through and just like that, the smiling image and the glittering portal vanish.

That's how it works. Each alternative past permits only one traveller and then collapses, lost forever. Some invention, huh?

A new image appears. Billy. My son. Alive. My heart thumps.

A hand on my arm. It's Em, nodding.

"Your turn."

Liam Hogan is an Oxford Physics graduate and award winning London based writer. His short story "Ana", appears in Best of British Science Fiction 2016 (NewCon Press) and his twisted fantasy collection, "Happy Ending Not Guaranteed", is published by Arachne Press. http://happyendingnotguaranteed.blogspot.co.uk, or tweet @LiamJHogan.

Pause

Matthew Stevens

Saniya clicked the button. The apple hung in mid-air. She sidestepped, careful not to touch it. In the foyer the mail was suspended as if by an invisible string from the mail slot. She chuckled as her Grandmama squatted over her favorite chair, stopped while sitting down, one leg and cane extended.

Saniya pressed the button again and grinned as the apple, the mail, and Grandmama dropped to their respective places. Unfrozen. Unaware.

Hmmm. What was the range of this thing?

She stepped outside. *Click!*

Car, cat, bird, a neighbor. Stopped cold.

This was going to be a fun summer.

Matthew Stevens spent years dreaming about being a writer before he found time late at night after the house was asleep to create characters and worlds and the stories for them to inhabit. During the daylight hours, he balances many jobs; husband, stay-at-home dad, server at a local brew pub, and all-encompassing geek. His current projects find him dabbling in a wide range of genres from his drafted novel, a paranormal thriller, to numerous fantasy and sci-fi shorts, along with an occasional blog post examining his perspective on his own writing journey and any intriguing geeky topic that catches his attention. He can be found online at:

Facebook: https://www.facebook.com/matthewstevensauthor
Twitter: @matt_the_writer
Blog: thedgeofeverything.wordpress.com

The Case of the Unliving Immortal

Matthew Yates

When Michael Winthrop fell into a coma in 1983 there wasn't much notable about it. A tragic accident, a fall at his father's construction site. When his twentieth birthday came in 1999 it was more remarkable, few patients had ever maintained brain or bodily function that long. When his father passed in 2008, his mother Shauna decided it was too remarkable to be left unremarked upon. When the documentary got made in 2019 he was still asleep. Healthy. When his mother died in 2050 – still healthy. When his brother died in 2076. His nephew in 2122. 2158. 2270. Always healthy.

Matthew Yates is an artist and poet from western Kentucky. His work can be found in/forthcoming in Memoir Mixtapes, Rhythm & Bones Lit, and Barren Magazine.

Lethal Salvation

Neel Trivedi

Tick. Tick. Tick.

Just five more minutes till I achieve what Buddhists call enlightenment.

Tick. Tick. Tick.

Eternal salvation.

Tick. Tick. Tick.

Free from depression.

Tick. Tick. Tick.

A childhood ambition.

Tick. Tick. Tick.

Suicide was deemed cowardly.

Tick. Tick. Tick.

So I chose another way. I copied Jeffrey Dahmer's actions and hoped for the best.

Tick. Tick. Tick.

Or worst. However one sees it.

Tick. Tick. Tick.

It worked. I'll thank him when I see him soon. As soon as what *they* call the lethal injection completely spreads in a few more seconds.

Tick. Tick. Tick.

Freedom at last!

Neel Trivedi is a freelance journalist and in the advertising business. He writes poetry and fiction. His work has been featured in Drabblez Magazine and Rhythm & Bones. He can be reached on Twitter at @Neelt2001.

Too Lazy to Panic

Patrick Stahl

The 2nd Marine Unit dissolved yesterday. You know, like sodium dissolves in water. Except with more blood. And corpses.

Anyway, it looks like my return planetside will be delayed. The invaders are within five hundred kilometers of the orbital base. That means they'll be here in twenty-six minutes, plus or minus several seconds.

Let's see: two minutes to the emergency armory, nine to don a flight suit in heavy traffic, five to reach the hangar, four to enter a fighter. That gives me six minutes to figure out how to fly it. Why did I sleep through those classes again?

Patrick Stahl is an undergraduate student at the University of Pittsburgh-Johnstown, where he studies Creative Writing, Multimedia, and French. He hopes to be able to study the development of speculative fiction, through an academic lens, in the near future.

Surviving Seaglass

Sara Codair

She strokes a shard of blue glass, a frozen gem, reflecting light from the dying sun. It was sharp once, but the raging ocean pounded its edges smooth.

Tracing the outlines of strange symbols, she sees the object's last interaction with humanity:

A rag-clad woman slashes her wrist. Blood pours out with sorrow, transforming cracked concrete to a crimson sea.

Shuddering, she pockets the beach glass. It's a window through time, a relic of the world that lived and died before her kind rose out of the ashes, and an artifact of the flawed beings that burned her phoenix planet.

Sara Codair lives on a lake in Massachusetts with a cat, Goose, who "edits" their work by deleting entire pages. Their debut novel, *Power Surge*, will be published by NineStar Press on Oct. 1, 2018. Find Sara online at https://saracodair.com/.

Press Enter?

David J. Wing

SCHEMATICS LOADED.

DO YOU WISH TO PROCEED…?

Sitting there, his finger hovering over the 'ENTER' button Kyle stood up and walked to the window.

The sky ripped at itself continually as the weather tore holes in every structure still standing.

Kyle stared through the cockpit and observed the near end, and he knew that if he was to hit that button, it was now or never.

The power would end within minutes, the tsunami approached and the chance would soon be gone…but it still nagged at him…the 'What ifs' and the 'What happens'…

The waves made his choice.

The Shrouded Women

Andrea Allison

I walked through the door heavy with a week's worth of mail and a few bags of groceries. They slipped from my fingers when my eyes met with theirs. Women. Dozens of them dressed in black shrouds hanging from my ceiling. I tried to blink away the horror but they remained, twisting and turning from their nooses.

Tears pooled in my eyes as a single piece of paper floated down before me. Six words staring up at me: "You can stop this. Don't quit." They vanished as all my doubts faded away. Winning the Senate seat will save us all.

Andrea Allison currently writes and resides in a small Oklahoman town. You can follow her on Twitter at @sthrnwriter.

Life: Spoiled by Cure

Alexandra Balasa

Mechaleg gears: rusted, mobility impeded by fifty percent. Call RoboCure on mindview, place new order. Remove shinplates, insert new gears. Repeat mantra: posthuman, not posthumous.

System malfunction: homeostasis disrupted, abnormal positive feedback loop. Buy HomeoStabilizers, send complaint for insufficient warranty. Install stabilizers, recycle old parts. Repeat mantra: garnished, not tarnished.

Available: Smartware chip upgrade, RoboCure promotion for regular customers. Retract complaint, upgrade mental software. Renew life expectancy calculation, five year increase. Repeat mantra: sustained, not stained.

Customer survey: rate satisfaction, respond to RoboCure questionnaire. Cured of all ailments, but satisfaction low. Dopamine regulators faulty, Joychip replacements never arrived. Mantras forgotten.

Alexandra Balasa attends the University of Texas at Dallas, where she is a teaching assistant and PhD student in literature and creative writing. Although she ponders existentialism, is obsessed with owls, and collects rocks, she promises she is not a cliché. After all, she does not own any cats (the neighbour's cats, who have appropriated her house, don't count). She writes speculative fiction with a psychological edge, and her writing explores questions of identity and moral ambiguity. Her writing has appeared in venues such as PodCastle, Cosmic Roots and Eldritch Shores, and Deep Magic. @BalasaAl.

You're Infinite

Andy Graff

You worry about death. Why, when there are infinite dimensions with infinite possibilities? In one, you're a warrior; in another, transgender. You lost your ears and nose to flesh-eating arachnids. You've uploaded your consciousness to the cloud, exploded from diarrhea. You've loved, lost, gained, hated, and loved again. You've cured cancer and caused cancer. You are a champion and a tyrant. You've served, gotten lost, and visited Proxima Centauri. You've cooked and traveled and saved and flown. Somewhere, you're forever. You are a collection of the infinite yous. You are everything you can imagine. There are no ends. Just you.

Andy Graff is a middle school language arts and creative writing teacher nestled among the high desert mountains of Utah. His writing was once praised by his mother. He is a massive soccer fan and a senior writer for RSL Soapbox on SBNation. His story, *Hadley's Aesthetics,* appears in Exoplanet Magazine. Most of the ideas for his writing come on the back of his bicycle as he crawls up mountain roads and sometimes crashes. He enjoys cheese. You can find him on Facebook and on Twitter.

The Theoretical Physicist Comes to Visit

Wilfred Cabrera

She only wanted twenty-four hours.

I welcomed the elderly stranger into my apartment, not knowing who she was. Punctured a wormhole, she explained, the first scientist to do so.

I had died, she said, in a limousine crash en route to our honeymoon. She never did remarry, instead working day and night to uncover a passage connecting our boundless realities.

Twenty-four hours was all I gave her. Took her out to dinner, then watched a movie. Let her sleep on the couch.

She would leave the next day. Return to her reality, where memories of her past hold more significance.

Hailing from Metro Manila, the Philippines, **Wilfred Cabrera** holds a degree in Literature and is currently pursuing an MFA in creative writing. His short fiction has appeared in *Literary Orphans*, *LONTAR: The Journal of Southeast Asian Speculative Fiction*, and *Philippine Speculative Fiction*. When he is not reading or writing, he enjoys playing video games and watching movies. Follow him on Twitter at @wilfredxcabrera.

Time's Up

Tianna Grosch

The time had come. Lucy had been waiting for it. Damn superstitions of the crew. Her legs trembled as she walked the plank, wooden board quivering beneath her weight. Lucy stiffened her back so they wouldn't see the way she shook. Behind her, tips of their drawn swords glinted in fading light - a thicket of thorns. White undergarments whipped around her legs. The crew began chanting. "Time's up, time's up." Time was a silly concept to Lucy, always had been. Yet, there was no escaping the inevitable. She took the final step and plunged toward the depths of the ocean.

Tianna Grosch has been writing her whole life and received her MFA at Arcadia University last year. She works as Assistant Editor at Times Publishing Newspapers, publishing 10 community papers a month. Tianna is working on a debut novel about women who survive trauma as well as a memoir. Her work has previously appeared or is forthcoming in Ellipsis Zine, Crack the Spine, Burning House Press, Who Writes Short Shorts, New Pop Lit, Blanket Sea Magazine, Echo Lit Mag and Nabu Review (both lit mags of Paragon Press), among others. In her free time she gardens on her family farm and dreams up dark fiction. Follow her on Twitter @tianng92 or check out her writing on CreativeTianna.com.

Long Distance Relationship

Rickey Rivers Jr.

[Earth] My dearest, I do long for your company. It bothers me deeply that we have yet to meet again. I await you every hour.

[Mars] My darling, I do understand. The pain that you feel hurts me as well. I promise to find a way.

[Earth] My dearest, my hearts pains for you, long into the night. Do say you will arrive soon.

[Mars] My darling, I have made plans for arrival. We shall reunite at last.

[Earth] Is it a dream? I cannot believe it true.

[Mars] It's true, a one year journey.

[Earth] Eternity, by another name.

Rickey Rivers Jr was born and raised in Mobile Alabama. He is a writer and cancer survivor. He likes a lot of stuff. You don't care about the details. He has been previously published in Every Day Fiction, Fiction365, Fabula Argentea, ARTPOST magazine (among other publications). Check out some stuff from him here, https://storiesyoumightlike.wordpress.com/. You may or may not find something you like there and that's a promise. Also, storiesyoumightlike (@storiesyoumight) | Twitter.

Another Day in Fairbanks

Joshua Scully

A tired couple stepped up to the ticket window in the Fairbanks Depot. Their appearance was bizarrely disheveled and fatigued.

"We need two tickets to Anchorage," the man croaked.

"That train doesn't leave until 8:15am," the teller warned.

"Never mind that," the woman barked. "Two tickets!"

After the transaction, the pair huddled on a bench.

"The tickets say 'July 18th'," the man whispered. "It's still July 18th!"

"Not a day has passed," the woman replied, "and this time we're inside the station. This time we'll get on the train!"

The man offered a pensive glance to his watch.

"And then?"

Joshua Scully is an American History educator and author of speculative fiction from Pennsylvania. His work can be found on Twitter @jojascully or online at www.jjscully.wordpress.com.

Meander

Brian Cody

Vinja jumped, no destination in mind, and looked around. Her thirtieth birthday party. The Gull. She'd only visited four or five times before, none recently. Rather than staying inside to hear two friends drunkenly debate the necessity of sleep, she wandered as far to the edge of the memory as she could - the street outside the bar. Vinja tired of endlessly roaming her own past, but being momentarily alone, away from the party, felt rejuvenated. Smiling, she turned towards the bar. A van swerved towards her. She didn't flinch, there was no need - but she closed her eyes in hope.

Brian Cody is a Florida native, now relocated to beautiful Chicago and working in tech. This is Brian's first drabble - you might say he's dabbling in drabbling.

The Time Mask

Aditya Deshmukh

Jonathan adjusted straps of the Time Mask. "I'm ready."

"I hope this works." Maria inserted platinum rods in his brain and shot electricity through him. "The Mask will now help your subconscious interact with dark energy."

When Jonathan opened his eyes, the red land of Mars was gone. He was alone in a gigantic network of dark energy lines that held the secrets of the universe.

As Jonathan touched the dark energy, Mars' history filled his mind. He saw life evolving on Mars, glorious civilizations, then fall of the planet and escape of the Martians to Earth. "We're fucking Martians!"

I'm a dark fiction writer and my works have appeared in Flashpoint, Drabbledark, Dastaan World Magazine, Martian Magazine, Letters Never series. My horror novelette will be published in August by Scarlet Leaf Review, and Treasure Chest anthology. Recently, I made it to the Top Ten Winners list of *Write India Campaign*, the biggest short story contest in India hosted by *Times of India*, the most reputed press in the country.

An Untimely Death

C. H. Williams

Adam spun the wheel hoping for the maximum allowance; a lifetime to change. Infinite options ticked by as the generator decided his fate. He could have thirty years or thirty minutes. From the moment of death, he would work backwards in time to fix his mistakes and change his life's course.

He gasped. It couldn't be. He had exactly four seconds to alter his story.

Four seconds was all it took to fall 220 feet to the water beneath the Golden Gate Bridge.

His body rose from the depths. Four seconds, three, two, one.

He stepped back from the ledge.

C.H. Williams is a full-time mum who predominantly writes women's fiction but dabbles in short stories and flash pieces as well. She can often be found with a jar of peanut butter in one hand and a bar of dark chocolate in the other, which coincidentally makes it rather difficult to type.

Heal All My Wounds

Eric Lewis

I knew cryosleep was right for me when I heard of it! All my problems would disappear with time. In the future my weight problems will be solved with, like, a pill. And I know future people will appreciate my unique personality, not like now. Job skills? More suited to a technologically advanced setting, and certainly in the future my intellect will be more attractive to women. But these people...I dunno. After I woke up, doctors said the same crap as before. Sensible diet, exercise? No pill, really? I could always go back into cryosleep. Maybe another couple centuries…

I am an organic chemist in the New England area, navigating the latest rounds of layoffs and still learning how to be a person again after surviving grad school. My short fiction has been published in Nature Futures (an SFWA-qualifying market), Electric Spec, Bards and Sages Quarterly, Allegory, Devilfish Review, the anthologies Into Darkness Peering and Best Indie Spec Fiction Vol 1, and multiple online venues detailed at https://ericlewis.ink/.

A Matter of Time

AD Nello

As the doctor takes one last look at my throat, another brick bounces off the window.

"Ignore them. It's reinforced. They would need a wrecking ball to get through."

I understand protesting when you have nothing to lose, but my life is on the line. I don't think it's a moral issue to use the timestream to save myself.

They're my stem cells, so I don't see why it's a problem.

Just as I'm about to go under, I struggle to ask a question.

"Hey Doc, isn't it strange...that these diseases cropped up just as the timestream opened up..."

When **AD Nello** isn't waiting for a green bar to fill while your application installs, uninstalls or updates - he writes sci-fi pulp from the too hot or too cold climates of Toronto. You can find out what he's working on now at adnello.ca.

The Prophecy of Byrek

Stuart Conover

The hooves of Zenlan's horse beat against the ground.

There was no time to spare.

The seer had spoken.

A child would be born in the village of Gulak.

A hybrid bastard spawn of an ogre and a dark elf.

Raw strength that would match with pure cunning.

This was one of three prophesized who could prevent him from ruling this world.

Zenlan could not allow it to survive.

It would cry out for the first time at nightfall.

He would make sure it was also the whelp's last.

Zenlan wouldn't know for decades.

Two half-breeds were born that night.

Stuart Conover is a father, husband, rescue dog owner, horror author, blogger, journalist, horror enthusiast, comic book geek, science fiction junkie, and IT professional. With all of that to cram in on a daily basis, it is highly debatable that he ever is able to sleep and rumors have him attached to an IV drip of caffeine to get through most days.

A resident in the suburbs of Chicago (and once upon a time in the city) most of Stuart's fiction takes place in the Midwest if not the Windy City itself. From downtown to the suburbs to the cornfields - the area is ripe for urban horror of all facets.

Homepage: http://www.StuartConover.com

Twitter: http://www.twitter.com/StuartConover

Facebook: https://www.facebook.com/StuartConoverAuthor

A Vocation

Stella Turner

"It's just a clutch bag" she yelled.

Yesterday it was just shoes, the day before just a dress

"Alison it's the last of our money" he yelled back. "Can't you understand, there is no money left?"

Relief swept through her, like the most intense orgasm. Three years to get through his trust fund, hard work spending it all on meaningless trinkets but she'd done it. She couldn't wait to report back to her boss! Jeff was so boring! The Devil makes work for idle hands but that wasn't true she loved her job. She would be rewarded abundantly in Hell.

Stella Turner was 'sent to Coventry', England at birth, loves Lady Godiva, the two cathedrals and all its history. Published in several anthologies and hopes to write a best-seller one day which may or may not get published. She just needs to write a few more words than her usual Flashes and Drabbles. Can be found on twitter @stellakateT.

Unraveled

Alexa Pukall

She walked backwards through time. Felt the profound loss of a loved one years before she met them; suffered tearful break-ups followed by first tense silences and then enchanted bliss.

Sometimes she thought it made her value life more - knowing who she was going to lose, and how soon. Other times it was harder to care. That exciting new friend? She'd lost all contact with them only six months ago.

It wasn't a lonely life. She had friends, lovers, family. But it broke her heart, sometimes, that in all the years unraveling before her, she'd never met anyone like her.

Alexa Pukall was born and raised in Germany. She studied Creative Writing at Chapman University, CA, where she refined her taste for fantasy, science fiction, and magic realism. After traveling the world for several years, she now pursues the writing life in Berlin.

Undoing Life's Choices

Heather Ewings

"Ready?"

Walter nodded. "Am I ever."

They approached the children playing in the yard.

"Daddy's home!" The excited squeals were well worth the gut-churning journey in the time-machine, the struggle to convince his younger self not to make those terrible choices.

It took Walter time to recognise the man embracing his children; the face unmarked by anger, himself, after a different life.

"I don't understand."

"You wanted your family to have the loving father and husband they deserve. You sent your life took a different course."

Walter's skin tingled, and he realised his body was fading.

"You no longer exist."

Heather Ewings is a Tasmanian author who writes in stolen moments between homeschooling two primary aged children and chasing after an active toddler. More information about Heather's stories can be found at www.heatherewings.com.

Dinner: Thirty-seven

Joaquin Fernandez

Just as she had thirty-six times before, The Executive materialized on the roof of the restaurant. As usual, her salad arrived just as a younger version of herself and her husband sat at their usual table. Would they have stayed so in love had he not died?

She gulped wine and watched them eat at the last restaurant they would ever go to. Every time he passed her on his way to the bathroom, The Executive caught his eye and he smiled at her the same way he had on the day they met. The same way he always would.

Joaquin Fernandez is a recovering filmmaker, constant wanderer, and Miami native. His work can be found in AFTERMATH as well as Rhythm & Bones. He is currently working on his first novel.

Time's Up

Irene Montaner

The rock lit the sky as it cut and burnt through the atmosphere. The moment it impacted on Earth the visions began.

Felled trees. Burning forests. Barren plains. Polluted rivers. Dying wildlife. And all sorts of weird landscapes that didn't happen naturally.

The new king was an insignificant creature that even didn't exist yet. Vulnerable alone but cunning. And reproduced itself like a virus. A new tyrant on Earth.

A hot wave of dust slapped the T-Rex on his face. It had seen too much and suddenly felt weak. It roared one last time and lay down to sleep. Forever.

Irene Montaner was born in sunny Tenerife. After having studied and/or worked in several rainy countries she realised she didn't really like the rain and moved to sunny Switzerland.

A graduate in Mathematics, she has put her degree to good use by writing speculative fiction. Her stories have appeared at 365 tomorrows and Every Day Fiction, among other venues.

No Friendly Drop

Liam Hogan

"There must be a way!" J begged Professor Laurence.

"To go back in time? It won't help."

"But I'll save R! Stop him taking the poison."

The scientist shook her head. "You can't appear in the same place twice. What would that do to reality?"

"Earlier then. I won't take your damned sleeping potion."

"Then you'll end up married--to another."

J shuddered. "The letter! I'll make sure the letter arrives!"

"In which case, this scene never happens."

"Can't you do *anything*?" J wailed.

"Hush, child. At least I can take away your pain."

In the candlelight the dagger glinted.

Liam Hogan is an Oxford Physics graduate and award winning London based writer. His short story "Ana", appears in Best of British Science Fiction 2016 (NewCon Press) and his twisted fantasy collection, "Happy Ending Not Guaranteed", is published by Arachne Press. http://happyendingnotguaranteed.blogspot.co.uk, or tweet @LiamJHogan.

Beyond the Known

Madison McSweeney

As a child, I read of explorers and scientists, fantastical devices invented and remote places uncovered– and I wept, for I knew that wonders beyond my imagination would be revealed long after my death.

And that is why I have created this machine.

I first travelled five, ten, fifty years into the future, and found progress slow. Finally, I leapt forward one hundred years.

In the far future, I found a grey river and a black-cloaked spectre, beckoning to me.

It seems each of us is only permitted to see so many years - and I had exceeded my allotment.

Madison McSweeney is a writer and poet from Ottawa, Canada.

She has published horror, science fiction, and fantasy stories in *Rhythm & Bones Lit*, *Deadman's Tome*, *Unnerving Magazine*, *Women in Horror Annual Vol. 2*, and *Dark Horizons: An Anthology of Dark Science Fiction*, as well as *Zombie Punks F*** Off* (due for release later this year) and the upcoming summer issue of *Polar Borealis*. Her poetry has appeared in *The Fulcrum, Bywords*, and in the forthcoming *Cockroach Conservatory, Vol. 1*.

She blogs at madisonmcsweeney.com, mainly about genre fiction and the Canadian music scene.

Djinn and Tonic

Sara Codair

I spent a millennium trapped in this cursed tonic bottle.

Unbelievable!

My ancestors spread beautiful lies about humans getting rich off the wishes we granted. I thought greedy mortals would free me, ignorant of why their predecessors trapped me in the first place.

Logic overpowered greed in a surprising number of humans.

Hundreds handled my bottle before one was dumb enough to let me out.

The fool!

I still taste his blood on my tongue and hear his screams echoing through my ears. It was the first meal I'd had in two centuries, and my hunger is far from sated.

Sara Codair lives on a lake in Massachusetts with a cat, Goose, who "edits" their work by deleting entire pages. Their debut novel, *Power Surge*, will be published by NineStar Press on Oct. 1, 2018. Find Sara online at https://saracodair.com/.

Ferryman

M. Yzmore

I keep seeking a place, a time, where someone, anyone, knows how to cure you, my love.

Each wormhole I travel reminds me of Styx, the river that separates the dead from the living. To cross, I must pay, but the Ferryman won't take coins.

I've lost an ear. Most teeth. Gallbladder. Spleen. Half of my fingers and half of my toes. Testicles. Kidney. Almost all hope.

Then I lost an eye and finally saw there's even less left of you than there's of me.

It's time to cross the Styx, my love. I have some coins for the Ferryman.

Maura Yzmore writes short-form literary and speculative fiction, as well as humor. Her recent work can be found in Asymmetry, Exoplanet, Occulum, and elsewhere. Find out more at https://maurayzmore.com or on Twitter @MauraYzmore.

An Endless Punishment

Hollie Adams

Endless streaks of blood tainted the stream from the skull dashed against the rocks. Two teenagers stood. Their breath was ragged, and their shoulders heaved as they squeezed the weapon in their hands. They did not say a word. Instead, they grabbed their stepmother's limp body and pushed her into the stream. Relief washed over them until the moment transformed and they were dashing their stepmother's brains out again. They had heard about this; the loop that the government had created, where all murderers would be forced to relive their crime, forever. Now they were a part of the loop.

Hollie Adams is an editor and owns the book review blog, *Foxtrevert.wordpress.com*, where she reviews early copies of books for a range of publishers. Her blog will be featured in an upcoming blog tour for Legend Press, London at the end of August. Hollie is currently working on her first novel and her fiction ranges from dark children's fiction and fantasy to animal literature focusing on British and Irish wildlife. Originally from North Yorkshire, England, Hollie spent ten years in Ireland and now lives in Stockholm, Sweden.

We All Noticed It

Emma De Vito

We all noticed it that day. A stillness. The air hung limply – occasionally interrupted by the wind which grappled with trees and tossed roof tiles, easing them free. At the time, it was just a hurricane – we were used to them; but never on this scale. And never simultaneously across the world.

The searing crimson sun had been the first signal.

'How bizarre'.

'Look at that!'

Yes, we all noticed it that day but did nothing. Gradually, they perished, but for those who understood and prepared for what was to come.

Ignorance is bliss. But it can also be deadly.

Originally from the West Midlands, but now living in Northampton, **Emma De Vito** is an English teacher and aspiring flash fiction and short story writer. In 2016, she co-founded a writing group in her local area and has recently got involved with The Word Factory as a Social Media Associate.

7:47

Kelly Matsuura

"$4.77, right?" I pay for my latte, then check my boarding pass. Gate 77, Seat 4G.

7-7-4. Third time today. Seven is universally lucky; four means 'death' in Japan. Get on the plane? *Don't* get on the plane?

I go to the gate. The damn plane is a 747! *Fourth time*…that decides it.

When the plane takes off, I'm in a taxi.

7:46. Traffic is slow. I close my eyes…

A loud explosion slams my ears and rattles the car. I stick my head out the window, in time to see a burning Skipper hurtling down towards me.

Kelly Matsuura grew up in Victoria, Australia, but always dreamed she would live abroad. She has lived in northern China and Michigan in the US, and over ten years in Nagoya, Japan, where she now lives permanently.

Kelly has published numerous short stories online; in group anthologies; and in several self-published anthologies. Her speculative fiction has been published by *Visibility Fiction, Crushing Hearts & Black Butterfly Publishing, A Murder of Storytellers*, and *Ink and Locket Press*.

As the creator and editor for *The Insignia Series*, Kelly uses her knowledge of Asian cultures to help other indie authors produce great diverse stories and to share the group's work with a new audience.

Blog: www.blackwingsandwhitepaper.com

Facebook: Kelly Matsuura/Kelly Noro Author

Twitter: Kelly Matsuura

The Insignia Series blog: www.insigniastories.com

Calendar Girl

Mike Murphy

A calendar.

That's what was inside the envelope from her ex. Gwen tacked it up in her bedroom. Pretty pictures. She may as well use it, even though it was from him. Tomorrow *was* the start of a new year.

#

She slept fitfully – running fevers, clutching and discarding blankets. The calendar pages flipped back and forth on their own, rushing the seasons outside.

The turning pages became a blur. Gwen's aching bones grated against each other for hours. She awoke seconds before, like kindling, they caught fire.

#

Nearby, her ex smiled at his chemistry set when he heard the sirens.

Mike Murphy has had over 150 audio plays produced in the U.S. and overseas. He's won five Moondance International Film Festival awards in their TV pilot, audio play, short screenplay, and short story categories.

His prose work has appeared in several magazines and anthologies. In 2015, his script "The Candy Man" was produced as a short film under the title DARK CHOCOLATE. In 2013, he won the inaugural Marion Thauer Brown Audio Drama Scriptwriting Competition.

Mike keeps a blog at audioauthor.blogspot.com.

45's Time Machine

S. E. Casey

Number 1 lost to 4. Number 4 was bested by 7.

Jackson dispatched Harrison easily. His next fight was surprisedly a doozy, the smaller number 10 biting and scratching. Jackson eventually prevailed sending an unconscious Tyler back through the portal.

Number 16 was brought forward from his time. Wrestling skills equal to his legend, Lincoln twisted Jackson into submission.

Behind the tinted glass of the private balcony, two men watched.

"Lincoln's a monster. You still sure about this 'Presidential Gauntlet' idea, Sir?"

The blonde-haired man stopped his stretching. "I'm the best. My victory will prove it. Then everyone will know."

Not long after celebrating his twenty years of accounting service in a Boston investment firm, **S.E. Casey** began to write. As an attempt to quell an unspecific desperation and stave off a growing resentment of *everything*, he found stories buried in the unlikely between-spaces of numbers, balances, and accounting formulae. This expanding existential collection has been published in many magazines and online publications, which can be found at www.secaseyauthor.wordpress.com.

Chronothanatos

Aislinn Batstone

God's timekeeping sucks. Rogues and cheats get extra play. My best friend Laura left the game – time out from serious injury.

With Laura gone, I hide in my room. My parents say I need time to grieve. I need science. The result, my timepiece, *Chronothanatos*, death of time. All it takes is a single hair.

Test subject: Mrs Carly Canker, ninth grade teacher, worst bully in the school.

Chronothanatos stops the game justly for a single player, red card for Mrs Canker. No more fouls. I insert the hair.

Someone has to think of the other players.

God never does.

Aislinn Batstone is an Australian writer of long and short-form fiction whose genre-bending tales have been published worldwide in anthologies and magazines including Stupefying Stories, Nature:Futures, Big Pulp, and many others. Discover more at www.aislinnbatstone.com.

A Lot Like Earth

Dennis Mombauer

They touch down on the planet and make camp near an estuary. The captain sends an expedition: a mercenary, a botanist, two geologists.

They march upriver through earthlike forest. No undergrowth, insects, or wind. At dusk, they reach a waterfall.

They climb up in the morning and discover the trails of four people. In the evening, they reach another cataract.

There are double the trails topside. The botanist feels followed. At the next waterfall, they set an ambush.

A day passes. At nightfall, their pursuers arrive: one mercenary, one botanist, two geologists.

They see each other, and the river stops.

Dennis Mombauer, *1984, currently lives in Colombo as a freelance writer of fiction, textual experiments, reviews, & essays on climate change & education. Co-publisher of "Die Novelle – Magazine for Experimentalism". Publications in various magazines & anthologies. German novel publication "Das Maskenhandwerk" (The Mask Trade) with AAVAA press in 2017. Homepage: www.dennismombauer.com.

The 'Just One Night' Conundrum

John Hoggard

Dorrie had always struggled with hyper-dimensional maths, but finally, it clicked.

His tutor seemed delighted and sent Dorrie upstairs to see the boss.

"So," he said to Father Christmas after a brief exchange of pleasantries, "you simply move between this universe and the parallel one where time runs backwards, thus, in this one, you deliver all the presents in one night?"

The man nodded.

"So how do you not age?" the boy asked.

Father Christmas leaned forward, stared intently at Dorrie.

Dorrie gasped. "You're Norrie, you graduated just last year!"

"And now you have your answer," Father Christmas replied, solemnly.

John Hoggard has been writing for as long as he can remember, his first publishing successes coming in the Hartlepool Mail "Chipper Club" aged 6. Since then he's continued to write mainly in the Science-Fiction and Fantasy genres, winning prizes for his "fan-fic" of the Star Trek franchise in his twenties at the various Conventions he attended.

John has also written several pieces of background fiction based on the game Oolite and his most popular work, Lazarus, serialised over 16 weeks, received over 15,500 viewings during that time. The E-book Anthology, Alien Items, featuring some of John's work (writing as DaddyHoggy), was released in early 2012.

In June 2012 John won the Biting Duck Press "Science in Fiction" Short Story Competition.

In November 2012, John's SF short story Baby Babble was included in the Anthology Fusion by Fantastic Books Publishing.

In October 2014 John contributed two pieces of flash fiction to a charity horror anthology, Ten Deadly Tales

In May 2016, John's had two SF short stories All in the Mind and The House was included in the Anthology Synthesis also by Fantastic Books Publishing.

John was most recently published in the horror anthology '666', where his 666-word story 'Headhunted' was highly commended by the editors of the anthology

In November 2017 John had five drabbles in an Official Elite: Dangerous Publication, Elite Encounters by David 'Selezen Lake' Hughes.

In June 2018 John had a drabble accepted into the new Science Fiction Magazine, The Martian Magazine, a new Science Fiction magazine currently specialising in the publication of drabbles.

John's main work in progress is a contemporary novel entitled Endless Possibilities about the world of Online Gaming and Science-Fiction Conventions. He is also working on a collection of 75-word short stories based on his successful contributions to the Paragraph Planet website and is working with illustrator Helen Withington to bring a selection of these stories to life.

Pride of the Fleet

Tyler McQuillan

The beginning, like the end, lacked in stature. Smeared points of light indicate the speed; without them, there is no motion. Cities cut swathes through the sky, inverted rudders without wakes. Predominant thought was that the empire was too large to fall. Physics will heel for our fleet, so strive onward!

The end came quickly, and in silence. The ocean swallowed the *Freestate* when it plummeted. Ten more joined it before the advance stopped. And again the slow voyage: another thousand years' retreat to return from a stillborn battle. The ships, demilitarized, freed from their dogma, took years in sinking.

Tyler McQuillan is a writer and poet from Western Mass and a grad from Western New England University's Creative Writing MFA. He is a passionate tutor that enjoys writing all sorts of fiction both long and short. He plays both the guitar and the ukulele and he's addicted to long words and old movies. More of his short fiction can be found at Medium.com/the-trove.

Cheers

Tiffany Michelle Brown

Margot and Stephanie tilted their stemless wine glasses back in unison. They wilted into the café-style chairs as the alcohol warmed them.

The women watched Adam, Margot's two-year-old, waddle across the checkerboard floor on chubby, unsure legs. His little-boy eyes grew wide with wonder as he approached a reflective, undulating oval.

Just before he giggled and stumbled through, Margot gestured to the rippling mass and sang, for the twentieth time that day, "Best purchase ever. Another glass, Steph?"

Stephanie grinned and nodded.

Adam laughed, tumbled through. The kitchen flickered.

Margot and Stephanie tilted their stemless wine glasses back in unison.

Tiffany Michelle Brown is a native of Phoenix, Arizona, who ran away from the desert to live near sunny San Diego beaches. Her work has been published by Fabula Argentea, Under the Gum Tree, Pen and Kink Publishing, and Shooter Literary Magazine. When she isn't writing, Tiffany can be found sipping whisky, practicing yoga, or reading graphic novels - sometimes all at once. Follow her adventures at tiffanymichellebrown.wordpress.com.

Relative Disaster

John H. Dromey

Scientists and lab techs crowded around a computer monitor's blank screen.

"Henri's been back for nearly an hour. What's the holdup with his written report? As our primary financial underwriter's eldest son, Henri's opinion carries a lot of weight."

"I'm told he's sneezing so much he can only key in one or two words a minute."

Finally, the screen lit up: *During my sojourn in the past, I learned I'm allergic to saber-tooth cats, dire wolves, wooly mammoths, dodo feathers and the pollen of too many extinct plants to mention. This project should be terminated. Time travel is sheer torture.*

John H. Dromey enjoys reading—mysteries especially—and writing in a variety of genres. He's had short fiction published in *Alfred Hitchcock's Mystery Magazine, Crimson Streets, Stupefying Stories Showcase*, and elsewhere, as well as in a number of anthologies, including *Chilling Horror Short Stories* (Flame Tree Publishing, 2015) and *Drabbledark: An Anthology of Dark Drabbles* (Shacklebound Books, 2018).

Finding Time

Hákon Gunnarsson

King Micheal entered the Time Keeper's lair with a quite agitated look on his face. "Is time slowing down?" the king asked.

"Yes, I'm afraid so," the Time Keeper answered without looking up from his books.

"Is there some problem with the time space continuum? Something that…"

"No, no, I just had to slow it down, hopefully it will only be temporary. I can't let it go on at the same pace."

"What do you mean? Why?"

The Time Keeper looked up. "Well, you've all been wasting too much time lately. So much so that I'm running out of time."

Hákon Gunnarsson is an Icelandic writer, who has written fiction, and nonfiction. Even though he did at one point want to become a novelist, he fell for the short story, and sticks mostly to that form. His work has appeared in literary journals, and anthologies in Icelandic, and English.

Stop Worrying

Eric Taylor

I've spent my life waiting to see four minutes pass.

I've seen men pry apart the hands of the clock and hold it back. Often beyond those four minutes.

But time, inevitably, marches forward. Things end. The clock will strike twelve. What remains after, though? What kind of dawn will humanity awaken to after midnight comes and goes? I've waited too long to care anymore. I've grown bored.

Using my influence, I just need to whisper, "Time's up."

I'll push the hands of the clock together myself, and I'll start with six simple words: "Mister President, you have to decide."

Eric Taylor is a writer from the Midwest. His inspirations and aspirations include the likes of Gaiman, Gibson, Lovecraft, and Spillane. He is on record as saying that you can have his Oxford Comma when you pry it from his cold, dead, and rigored hand.

That's What Happened to You

Laurence Raphael Brothers

Souls are only capable of moving so fast. Three or four hundred miles an hour, perhaps. Which is why it takes a while after a long air flight to feel like you're really there, wherever you are. All around us, the souls of people who have just flown long distances are racing by, following an etheric tropism to return to their bodies. Every once in a while, after a vacation or business trip, a soul gets lost and never finds their way back. Or they get confused and wind up in the wrong body. Yes. That's what happened to you.

Laurence Raphael Brothers is a writer and technologist with a background in AI R&D. He has recently published short stories in Nature Magazine, the New Haven Review, PodCastle, and Galaxy's Edge, among other markets. Visit his website to read more stories at https://laurencebrothers.com/ and follow him on twitter: @lbrothers.

There I Was

Joachim Heijndermans

Why did I shoot? Yeah, I panicked, but I could have taken a second to look. Then he wouldn't be dead.

"There you are," he said, like greeting an old friend. I was halfway in his safe when he startled me. I shot him before I got a chance to notice the birthmark on his face. My face. Ours.

Commotion. Security. No way out but the way I came.

I returned to my time, several grand richer and a future set in stone. I'd be forced to return in thirty-two years. I had an appointment with myself to keep.

Joachim Heijndermans writes, draws, and paints nearly every waking hour. Originally from the Netherlands, he's been all over the world, boring people by spouting random trivia about toys, comics and film. A graduate of the Kubert School in New Jersey, he works as a graphic designer and cartoonist. His work has been featured in a number of publications, such as Mad Scientist Journal, Asymmetry Fiction, Metaphorosis, Econoclash Review, the Gallery of Curiosities and Gathering Storm Magazine, and he's currently in the midst of completing his first children's book. You can find his work at www.joachimheijndermans.com, or follow him on Twitter: @jheijndermans.

The Scavengers of Lost Time

Russell Hemmell

Titan's washed-away reflection on the spaceport panels reminded Gillian of a squeezed orange over a monochrome tableware. Under her feet, the surface of Enceladus was as white as a funeral mausoleum. A mausoleum called home, space colony standards.

"Earth awaits." The Captain pointed at the pilot seat. "I'll retrieve Gothic artefacts and Corinthian marbles. You?"

Nothing remained of the once-Blue Planet but solar flares and submerged megalopolis. Deprived of humans, teeming with fish, a hunting ground for nostalgic souls.

She strapped herself on. "Seashells and broken hearts."

The Earth-bound Harvester shuttle lifted off, crossing Saturn's rings like a shooting star.

Russell Hemmell is a statistician and social scientist from Scotland, passionate about astrophysics and speculative fiction. Recent work in Aurealis, The Grievous Angel, New Myths, and others. Finalist in The Canopus 100 Year Starship Awards 2016-2017. Blog: earthianhivemind.net, Twitter handler: @SPBianchini.

Fifth Sun

Tianna Grosch

Jason pulled out a syringe filled with mercury-colored liquid thick like serum - thicker than blood. The needle's tip glinted in the sun. Aurora wondered if it would hurt breaking her skin.

"Just a pinch," Jason said, reading her thoughts. He squeezed her wrist, anchoring her arm in one fist. "After this, you can't travel back." His eyes burned with the intensity of his meaning.

This was permanent. No reverse. No do-overs.

She nodded. The needle bit deep.

Her world morphed, trees melted into ink puddles and Aurora felt her body sucked through a time warp, thrown amidst the unknown.

Tianna Grosch has been writing her whole life and received her MFA at Arcadia University last year. She works as Assistant Editor at Times Publishing Newspapers, publishing 10 community papers a month. Tianna is working on a debut novel about women who survive trauma as well as a memoir. Her work has previously appeared or is forthcoming in Ellipsis Zine, Crack the Spine, Burning House Press, Who Writes Short Shorts, New Pop Lit, Blanket Sea Magazine, Echo Lit Mag and Nabu Review (both lit mags of Paragon Press), among others. In her free time she gardens on her family farm and dreams up dark fiction. Follow her on Twitter @tianng92 or check out her writing on CreativeTianna.com.

Shoah

Renee Firer

Bodies press against Alter, smothering his small form beneath cloth and the choking scent of excrement.

Tugged free, the smell of lavender envelops him, tainted only by the dry smoke that clings like a virus to his mother's shirt. He closes his eyes and for a moment he is home, surrounded by his *ima's* delighted laugh and his *aba's* gruff, but happy murmurs.

One night, two months ago, they came for his father. He hadn't seen him since.

The brakes screech, and they tumble forward. The door opens and men shout, "Juden," as if it is a curse. They've arrived.

Renee Firer lives in the greater Philadelphia area and received her MFA from Arcadia University this past May. When she's not working on her novel, she's spoiling her puppies, losing her pens, and planning her next worldly adventure. Her work has previously appeared in *Teen Ink* and *Loco Mag.*

How Bad Could it Be?

Mikko Rauhala

Lauren stood in front of the mailbox, envelope in hand. It was an old-fashioned approach, but she was an old-fashioned girl. Hopefully John would appreciate the sentiment.

The postman interrupted her reverie: "I'm done emptying this. Did you want that in the bag?"

Shaking, Lauren handed him the envelope. There was no turning back now, but how bad could it be?

As the postman drove off, a flash of light next to the mailbox startled Lauren. There stood an older woman with a vague resemblance to Lauren's mother, frantically looking around.

"Double-check the calibration!" she shouted at Lauren before disappearing.

Mikko Rauhala is a speculative fiction writer from Finland. His English debut story, The Guardian of Kobayashi, is featured in the anthology Never Stop. His flash fiction may be found in Drabbledark, The Self-Inflicted Relative, and on 101words.org.

Food as Faith

Jonathan Ficke

They should not have given me access to the time machine.

In 2017, a member of an isolated religious order opened a pop up restaurant in New York City. It lasted for one night, and one night only. To a person, everyone described it as transcendent, life-changing, divine. I missed it.

While everyone argued over how to use it -- prevent a war? Kill a dictator? Visit lost wonders of the world? Seek out the origins of world religions? -- I made my move.

With a watering mouth and growling stomach, I skipped backward in time on my own personal gastronomic pilgrimage.

My work has previously appeared in <u>Writers of the Future, Vol 34</u>, <u>Tales of Ruma</u>, and is forthcoming from <u>Martian</u>.

Meddlesome

Matthew Stevens

My watch had stopped. No matter. Time was irrelevant. Travelling backward or forward with ease. Mistakes could be erased. Wrongs righted.

But where to start? Eliminate a dictator? Rescue a visionary? I would be famous. Or maybe, I could slip in and out of time, remaining a secret; an enigma for conspiracy theorists to puzzle out.

A crack split the air. I searched for the origin.

Bang! My chest exploded with intense pain. Blood soaked my shirt.

"I'm sorry. It's for the best," my own voice apologized. Sincerely.

I focused on a figure and watched as I lowered a pistol.

Matthew Stevens spent years dreaming about being a writer before he found time late at night after the house was asleep to create characters and worlds and the stories for them to inhabit. During the daylight hours, he balances many jobs; husband, stay-at-home dad, server at a local brew pub, and all-encompassing geek. His current projects find him dabbling in a wide range of genres from his drafted novel, a paranormal thriller, to numerous fantasy and sci-fi shorts, along with an occasional blog post examining his perspective on his own writing journey and any intriguing geeky topic that catches his attention. He can be found online at:

Facebook: https://www.facebook.com/matthewstevensauthor

Twitter: @matt_the_writer

Blog: thedgeofeverything.wordpress.com

Simon's Hourglass

Andrea Allison

The top chamber from Simon's hourglass slowly emptied, melting years off his life. He laid vacant in his bed as his end drew near. Glee boiled inside me watching the sand trickling down. He fought against his impending death, knowing my dark secret, but not a word of triumph escaped my lips.

He drew in his final wheezy breath and then nothing. A man of simple means transformed into the wealthiest in the world as his only heir. A smile spread across my face until a man in black appeared from the shadows. "His life is yours until your hourglass empties."

Andrea Allison currently writes and resides in a small Oklahoman town. You can follow her on Twitter at @sthrnwriter.

Effect & Cause

David Bernard

My spaceship hit something, triggering "safety protocols," also called "careening out of control while diagnostics place the engines off-line."

When engine control returned, I was already caught in the sun's gravity. I was about to become the first astronaut on the sun – unless I could slingshot around the sun.

It worked, but I was out of fuel, drifting helplessly. Suddenly I knew what happened next. I braced as my ship hit my ship. I watched as I went careening toward the sun. The slingshot had also created a time warp.

I've probably said it before - I hate causal loops.

David Bernard is a native New Englander who lives in South Florida, albeit under protest. His previous works include short stories in anthologies such as *Snowbound with Zombies* (Post Mortem Press), *Legacy of the Reanimator* (Chaosium), and *The Shadow over Deathlehem* (Grinning Skull Press).

Exit

Bart Van Goethem

Now traffic news: there's been an accident on the A45.

Oh-oh, Jason mumbled to himself.

A truck crashed into a car right before the exit to Birmingham.

Great, that's my exit.

Witnesses say the car just stalled, as if it broke down suddenly. The truck behind it couldn't avoid the crash. The right lane is now temporarily closed.

That's strange. There's no traffic jam.

The driver of the car didn't survive the collision.

Okay, I'm nearing the exit. There's no sign that anything just happened here. It's – wait, why's my oil light blinking all of a sudden?

Oh, shit.

Thricely

Stephen D. Rogers

That flicker you see is me, and that odd sound a bit of my message, repeated in hopes you can piece it together.

Please forgive me for stealing your time machine before learning how to use it. I only wanted to watch you build the device.

Please forgive me for stealing your time machine before learning how to use it. I only wanted to watch you build the device.

Please forgive me for stealing your time machine before learning how to use it. I only wanted to watch you build the device.

Can you break me out of this loop?

Stephen D. Rogers is the author of more than 800 shorter works. His website, www.StephenDRogers.com, includes a list of new and upcoming titles as well as other timely information.

Geniuses Think Alike

Catherine J. Cole

If I had left myself be, I would not lie here dying; both attempted murderer and victim.

I planned to steal the life I had here because I missed Kaylee so much. My baby was alive in this time. Why couldn't I guess I was planning the same thing in some other Earth, where I'd also lost her?

Now I know at least two of me won a Nobel Prize. I thought burying myself in work would make me forget that sickness took my child. Couldn't I be happy that I had once had a daughter? Weren't the memories enough?

Catherine J. Cole won 1st prize in the Metamorphose Literary Science Fiction & Fantasy Short Fiction Contest. The winning story appeared in the anthology *Metamorphose Vol. 2.* More of her short fiction can be found in the magazines and anthologies *Candlesticks and Daggers: An Anthology of Mixed-Genre Mysteries*, *Fantasia Divinity Magazine's Distressing Damsels*, *One Hundred Voices Vol. 3*, and *Broadswords and Blasters Issue 6*. Ms. Cole has lived in the United States, France, and Colombia. When not writing, she works as a translator, which demands that she often work abroad, away from her family in Florida. Follow her on Twitter @CJCole2U and check out her website www.catherinejcole.com.

James in the Museum with the Revolver

Danny Beusch

There's a monthly school trip to the District's museum. On level 33, James reads the first plaque:

Cluedo, 'board game', manufactured District 12, 1949.

> *Part of the 'murder-mystery' genre, Cluedo was a by-product of post-Cartesian policing. This posited that any observable effect could be logically traced back to its origin; however, the development and refinement of affordable body-modification technologies in the mid-21st century challenged its hegemony, culminating in widespread civil disorder. Proactive law enforcement models were subsequently developed and implemented.*

James removes his headset, runs a finger around the cell door, waits for the Vitamin D lamps to turn on.

Danny Beusch tells stories, succinctly. His work can be found in *Paragraph Planet, Ellipsis Zine, The Cabinet of Heed, and Ink in Thirds*. Find him on twitter: @OhDannyBoyShhh

Time-consuming

Cherryl Chow

Hunger ravaged her.

The moonlight seeped in through the barred window.

The girl was scrawny, skeletal, starving. Stunted in her growth, she occupied less and less space as time passed. And yet, in just the last hour, she'd polished off a hog and a cow.

The door flew open; a dark-robed woman entered.

"Ma!" The girl mewled.

The woman held out a cleaver, as if mindful of spilling the reflected moon, carefully considering the only remedy that could possibly work. Carving the flesh from her own back, the woman tossed the bloody scrap to her daughter.

"Eat," commanded Mother Time.

Cherryl Chow lives in N. California with four cats, one husband, two pairs of missing shoes, and more books than she can count.

Permission Slip

I. E. Kneverday

The Z-30 safari-class hovercraft landed in the muddy field with an audible *plop*.

"I thought we weren't supposed to touch anything," Mr. Richmond squeaked in a nervous staccato.

The pilot ignored him.

"Dammit," she tried (and failed) to whisper while slamming a fist down onto the control panel. "Our active camouflage has failed, too."

The kids, overhearing this, erupted into a chorus of conjecture.

"Can they see us?" Suzie blurted.

"Are they going to kill us?" Timmy wondered aloud.

Outside, a trio of men adorned in metal breastplates was marching toward the hovercraft. A trio of crucifixes loomed behind them.

I. E. Kneverday is a writer of science fiction, horror, and fantasy. His short fiction has been featured in publications including *Drabbledark, Exoplanet Magazine*, and *101 Words*. Learn more at Kneverday.com and come say hi on Twitter (@Kneverday) and Facebook (facebook.com/kneverday).

Connected Through Time

Karen Heslop

Aneksi and Minnakht had been in love for eons. The Prophetess hadn't lied – they were soul-mates but she hadn't mentioned the tiring searches after each re-incarnation. The last time, they'd been separated by five years and two continents. They'd only enjoyed 10 years before death took her.

She'd followed her friends to a party to celebrate her 21st birthday and keep her mind occupied. A lanky wraith of a boy approached her.

"Wanna dance?"

"No thanks."

He moved closer.

"Y'sure?"

"She said no."

Aneksi turned towards the familiar voice, a smile brightening her face. They'd be together longer this time.

Karen Heslop writes from Kingston, Jamaica. Her stories can be found in Grievous Angel. Martian Magazine and The Future Fire among others. She tweets @kheslopwrites.

A New Life in Hermosillo

S. S. Sanderson

After throwing his bank cards and phone into the Santa Cruz River, he crossed the border at Nogales without incident. He drove for three and a half hours to Hermosillo with his remaining cash tucked into a back pocket.

He resisted a desire to call his mother from one of the public buildings and decided on a new name. He next set his mind on the business of destroying his automobile.

Hermosillo was an impressive city and surely possessed a chop shop. Once he had that finished, he'd have all the time in the world to begin his new life.

Oracle

Robert Wyndham

Some people had a gift: they saw the future. These oracles, however, couldn't change it. Just watch.

Alcaeus was one. A known eccentric, few people went to him. When I met with him, asking about a new business venture, he shrank away from me as if I had hit him, refusing answers.

That venture failed; I was ruined.

I thought I had only one path forward: banditry.

I waited one night near a footpath. Footsteps approached.

I sprang, my dagger slicing, and saw no rich somebody, only poor Alcaeus.

With his dying breath, he muttered, "Just like I saw it..."

Robert Wyndham has worked overseas in China as an English teacher and is currently a proofreader based near New York City.

Debt

Dan R. Arman

I am utterly bored by math, but paranoid about numbers.

On my right arm, a number scrolls relentlessly—my accrued debt. It's a mind-numbing, soul-crushing number that constantly rises—broken only by brief moments that pause the figure's climb towards oblivion.

It would be easy to become entranced and morbidly watch the number whirl, transform like a snake shedding its skin, only to swallow more of my arm. I have no time for that.

On my left arm, another number pulses and fades. It's this number that contingent workers obsess over. Watch for the number, get the time job, live another day.

---

https://danrarman.wixsite.com/likedreamersdo

Five Minutes can be a Lifetime

CR Smith

Billy watched Tom's bike while he popped inside for the latest comic. Books spilled from shelves and drifted across the floor.

Tom walked up and down the rows lost in the labyrinth, eventually exiting onto a street filled with flying cars, where people wore strange clothes and spoke an unrecognisable language.

He turned back. The bookshop had disappeared. With no means of returning he adapted to this new way of life.

Then one day, now an old man, Tom opened a door and walked out of the bookshop. Billy was still waiting there. Neither of them had aged one bit.

CR Smith is an artist and writer living in the UK. Her work has been published by Ellipsis Zine, Spelk Fiction, Visual Verse, Zeroflash and The Cabinet of Heed, and is to be found in several anthologies including, The Infernal Clock, Drabbledark: An Anthology of Dark Drabbles and 'Please Hear What I'm Not Saying'. There are also upcoming pieces in the Trembling With Fear anthology, The Infernal Clock Deadcades anthology and the Zeroflash anthology.

Twitter @carolrosalind
https://crsmith2016.wordpress.com
https://www.instagram.com/smith.cr/?hl=en

Nostalgiasaurus Wrecks

J. S. Deel

My PhD work on the philosophies of Dunne and Benjamin allowed for time-travel, of a sort: I discovered that images were frozen interfaces between past and present – wormholes, basically.

The Cretaceous was just as wild and verdant as it had been in my childhood picture-books, and it only took a home-made field generator and some hallucinogens to get there. Most importantly, the dinosaurs were cool monster-reptiles, and not goofy-looking feathered things. It was better than time-travel: this was the past as it *should have been.*

Then I gave them lasers and time-machines. So, the invasion's my fault, kind of. Sorry.

He is the editor of the Irish science fiction anthology *A Brilliant Void* (2018), and his translation work can be seen in *The Short Fiction of Flann O'Brien* (2013).

Stopping Time

Rebecca Thomas

Stopping time can be addictive. It only lasts a minute, but it's amazing how much you can do in sixty seconds.

It started as a joke, harmless pranks to mess with each other. But then it escalated. Turns out moving someone into a potentially precarious position takes very little time at all.

And you have to stay close...just in case. You wouldn't want to miss their bumbling and stumbling...or possible slip over the edge...and forgetting to catch him... It serves him right. First getting me fired...then evicted...and then crashing my car...

Bastard.

...fifty-seven ...fifty-eight...fifty-nine.

Rebecca Thomas is a wordsmith with an enthusiasm for science fiction and fantasy storytelling. A longtime writer, editor, and digital content creator, she channels her fascination with Clarke's Third law into writing short stories and novellas in various flavors of near future science fiction and contemporary fantasy. As her schedule permits, she enjoys using her keen eye and writing savvy to help other writers polish their own writing

Since completing a degree in education, she has used her extensive writing and curriculum design skills to create educational programs and guides for museums, live-action roleplaying games (LARPs), and nearly every job she's ever had. Currently, she is rebuilding her writing practice to better support her voiceover activities and her dreams of creating new and interactive media.

Last Attempt

Jack Wolfe Frost

I'm now back in 1956 and a doctor. This is my last attempt, I don't know anything else I can try.

I'm at my birth - I nearly died – umbilical cord strangulation. They say that's what probably caused the brain damage, and my resultant split personality.

I laugh quietly. Fortunately my name isn't Jekyll, though my other half I could certainly call Mr. Hyde.

"Stop!" I shout. "Something's wrong." The midwife glares at me – doctors are not normally present at home births.

I slide my hand up my mother's birth canal, find the umbilical cord and gently untangle it and

---

Jack Wolfe Frost is the Eternal Rebel; he rebels against everything which may have the word "rules" or "behave" within it. Born in Sheffield, UK, in 1956; he first started writing in 1982, as a hobby - Now older and wiser, he has had several poems and short stories published.

Paradox Paradise

R. Daniel Lester

The aliens arrived in 2134 and gifted us time travel tech on a silver platter. They'd been watching us for centuries like television, finally figuring we'd fucked up enough. They felt sorry for us.

So even aliens have egos and like to be admired and profusely thanked for their graciousness.

And sure, we could've treated time travel like surgery, only if necessary and only to cure the most important historical ills. But, of course, no--we abused it. A paradox paradise. The resultant timequakes ripped the world apart like lions on a downed gazelle.

We just can't have anything nice.

R. Daniel Lester's writing has appeared in print and online in multiple publications, including Adbusters, Geist, 365 Tomorrows, Broken Pencil, Pulp Literature and the Lascaux Prize Anthology. Recently his novella, *Dead Clown Blues* was shortlisted for a 2018 Arthur Ellis Awards for Best Crime Novella by the Crime Writers of Canada. The second book in the Carnegie Fitch Mystery Fiasco series, *40 Nickels,* will be released in May 2019.

Wasted Time

Jacob Stokes

"Is it time?"

"More like do we have the time...."

"There's time enough as long as we start on time."

"If we succeed then all of time will be ours."

"That's one theory. Your theory. My theory still remains that we'll be able to travel instantly outside of time constraints, and not that this will open the door to travel anytime within time."

"We'll soon see who is right because the time is... oh no."

"What?"

"The time. It's passed. We missed it. Our chance has passed this time. We'll have to wait on the next time it's all aligned."

Jacob Stokes is a lifelong reader and collector of books, primarily SciFi and Fantasy. He resides in Alabama with his wife, daughter, and puppy. He can be found on Twitter and Instagram by his username of RedStarReviews or at his website www.redstarreviews.com

Holdout

Phil Dyer

It's not the end of everything. The Local Group at most. The Universe crawls on, untroubled by a wound of fifty-odd galaxies. Plenty to spare.

Ultimate weapon my ass.

Way down here, it seems pretty ultimate. I'll give it that.

We're rationing our time. Not much. The bubble was planet sized at first. Then a country. City. Block. Now just this room.

Delaying tactics. The time in here is stale, recycled. I give my rallying speech again, ignoring the echo. Some people nod. One cries- still? Again? Maybe I alone remember.

We'll think of something yet.

We'll think of.

We'll.

Phil Dyer is a molecular biologist working in Liverpool, in the UK. His research often inspires his writing and he has plenty of time to think during long protocols.

65 Million Years of Mokele

Joshua Scully

"I didn't leave Lubumbashi to chase shadows!" the hunter shouted. "Where is mokele-mbembe? Where is this Congolese dinosaur?"

The translator shrugged, but the Turumbu guide remained confident. He handed the foreigner a spear and several colorful feathers.

"What's this?" the huntsman sneered. "Mokele-mbembe survives 65 million years in this jungle and I'm to down the beast with sticks and stones?"

The translator and the Turumbu spoke quickly.

"No," the translator said. "Mokele-mbembe made that spear and lost those feathers. A tribe of Mokele-mbembe live in the river basin."

"A tribe?" the hunter countered.

"Apparently 65 million years allow for advancement."

Joshua Scully is an American History educator and author of speculative fiction from Pennsylvania. His work can be found on Twitter @jojascully or online at www.jjscully.wordpress.com.

The Frozen Desert

Paul Thompson

Time catches up with us once more.

We run towards the safety of the hills, another time-stop due any minute. All around us we see plants no longer wavering in the breeze, clouds rolling to a halt, footsteps now silent as we run.

It catches Natasha first, freezing her mid-run, in a position that will leave her aching at the restart. I relax my limbs and drop to the floor, my position perfect for the stasis.

Four hours pass, statues in the frozen desert.

When time restarts we flex our limbs, snap our joints, and continue our run to safety.

Paul Thompson lives and works in Sheffield. His work has appeared in Ellipsis Zine, The Cabinet of Heed, and forthcoming in Spelk. Find out more @hombre_hompson

Time is A-changing

Maddy Hamley

The device buzzes, and I sigh. I never thought I'd miss digital clocks.

There are still some left, counting down in silence, along with an odd assortment of pocket watches and a single hourglass. But most of my work is now listed on a rectangular screen, names neatly aligned with dates. Ready for reaping on the buzzer.

What wouldn't I give for a good old candle. The scent of burning tallow fit the job so well. Or a solid, mahogany grandfather clock. Something substantial.

I'd even take another radiology experiment. I've still got a Geiger counter somewhere. The device buzzes.

Maddy Hamley has been published on Paragraph Planet and the London Independent Story Prize website (recommended writer in 2018 Q2), as well as in Sensorially Challenged Vol. 1 and Drabbledark. She should be working on her PhD but spends far too much time writing Twitter fiction as @nossorgs or enjoying Hamburg with her husband.

Trying to Make a Living

Patrick Stahl

I'll never forget the stories Grandpa used to tell about working in the steel mill. The labor was hard, but the wizards paid well: two hundred hours a week. He lived to the old age of seventy-four.

Pa griped about his work a lot. He started out in Grandpa's mill as a laborer, worked up the ladder, and was eventually promoted to foreman. Even then, he only earned one hundred and eighty hours. He passed at sixty-seven.

I got a call from my boss last night. I'm going to need a second job if I want to exist until retirement.

Patrick Stahl is an undergraduate student at the University of Pittsburgh-Johnstown, where he studies Creative Writing, Multimedia, and French. He hopes to be able to study the development of speculative fiction, through an academic lens, in the near future.

Ten Again

Maria Mazzenga

James peered at the label of the Aquafina bottle he'd pulled out of a box of beach toys stuffed in a corner of his recently deceased parents' basement. "Best By 8/13/1999," it read. He looked down at his watch--nineteen years ago. He screwed off the cap and put his mouth to the opening. As the expired water flowed down his throat, James tasted sea water, smelled salty air, and heard seagulls squawk. They were on vacation Virginia Beach. Dad was adding another bucket of sand to the castle they were making, while mom cheered them on from a blanket.

Maria Mazzenga writes poetry, novels, and history from her home in Arlington, Virginia. She serves as editor at <u>Open Arts Forum</u>, has most recently published poetry in The Amethyst Review, The Bitchin' Kitsch, and Eyedrum Periodically. She is currently at work on a sci-fi novel revolving around the origins of the Great Pacific Garbage Patch.

Mercy Killing of Civilization

Neel Trivedi

"Merely stepping on a single ant can alter centuries of history," the professor had repeatedly warned.

As did the writings of H.G. Wells and countless other movies and TV shows about time travel.

Just one question nagged Benjamin as he disposed of the professor's bloody body before settling down in his machine.

Why was that such a bad thing?

What had "history" given him anyway? A world full of rapists, racists, murderers and corrupt politicians!

Step on an ant? he thought as he adjusted the controls. *Screw that! I'll go ten times better and just kill Adam and Eve!*

Neel Trivedi is a freelance journalist and in the advertising business in Dallas, TX. He writes poetry and fiction. His work has been featured in Drabblez Magazine and Rhythm & Bones. He can be reached on Twitter at @Neelt2001.

The Mobius Veil

Matthew Yates

The repair expedition had only left fifteen minutes ago and already Mallart was sick. Crossing the Veil always makes him sick.

Today it's Knossos, 1763 BCE. The smell of fish and din of craft means prosperity for these people, but for Mallart it means vertigo.

He was only there as art expert and could scarcely focus on anything.

Hmm, yes, dolphins. Bulls, yes. Youths. Yes. Pianos.

Wait...

"Found the glitch!"

"We'll see..." "Shit yeah, a Steinway."

Mallart was positive this wasn't patchable; it'd require full diagnostics. Minoan civilization will collapse again this sequence; it always goes better when they don't.

Matthew Yates is an artist and poet from western Kentucky. His work can be found in/forthcoming in Memoir Mixtapes, Rhythm & Bones Lit, and Barren Magazine.

Fifteen Ghosts

Michael Carter

I set out to meet fifteen ghosts—representing the ratio of the dead to the living—who walked the Earth before me. For years I searched cemeteries, ghost towns, haunted houses, and crematoria. I traveled the world over many times, but, alas, I found no ghosts. Tired from my pursuits, I laid down to rest. When I woke, they appeared in a line starting at the foot of my bed. I rose and shook each of their hands. With a firm grip, the last ghost said, "Welcome, Number Sixteen. You died in the third world war; you will stand for the deceased."

Michael Carter is a short fiction and creative nonfiction writer who grew up reading an odd combination of sci-fi and Louis L'Amour westerns. He's also a ghostwriter in the legal profession and a Space Camp alum. He's online at www.michaelcarter.ink and @mcmichaelcarter.

Ten Minutes

Max Shephard

If I'd left right at nine, I wouldn't be here right now.

I was supposed to follow her to Oxford for the football game, a four hour trip, but at nine-ten, the wall clock beside my bed still read nine, a simple dead battery the culprit.

I called her to apologize, but she never answered.

There'd been a pile up on the interstate, vehicles mangled beyond recognition into formless chunks of metal and broken glass.

An eighteen-wheeler driver, distracted.

Her car and the one behind it, crushed.

Ten minutes late on a technicality, my heart died along with that battery.

Max Shephard is a Mississippi attorney, entrepreneur, and author who likes his coffee dark and his fiction darker. He stories have appeared on the Simply Scary Podcast and Creepypod and he is a regular contributor to Reddit's No Sleep forum under the username creeping_dread.

Afterword

Thank you for picking up a copy of *Chronos: An Anthology of Time Drabbles.* I hope you enjoyed this small collection of micro fiction. If you're interested in reading more drabble-length fiction, check out editor Eric S. Fomley's website ericfomley.com or follow him @PrinceGrimdark on Twitter.

Made in the USA
Coppell, TX
12 January 2020

14428061R00062